ONE BEAR
ALL ALONE
Caroline Bucknall

Dial Books for Young Readers · New York

To Gill
who made up the best rhymes

First published in the United States
by Dial Books for Young Readers
A Division of E.P. Dutton
A Division of New American Library
2 Park Avenue
New York, New York 10016
Published in Great Britain by Macmillan Publishers Ltd.
Copyright © 1985 by Caroline Bucknall
All rights reserved
U S
10 9 8 7 6 5 4 3 2 1

Library of Congress Cataloging in Publication Data
Bucknall, Caroline. One bear all alone.
Summary: Relates the activities of one two . . .
to ten bears during a busy day.
1. Children's stories, American.
[1. Bears—Fiction. 2. Stories in rhyme. 3. Counting.]
I. Title.
PZ8.3.B8490n 1985   [E]   85-6968
ISBN 0-8037-0238-8

The full-color artwork was prepared using black ink
and colored pencils. It was then camera-separated
and reproduced as red, blue, yellow, and black halftones.

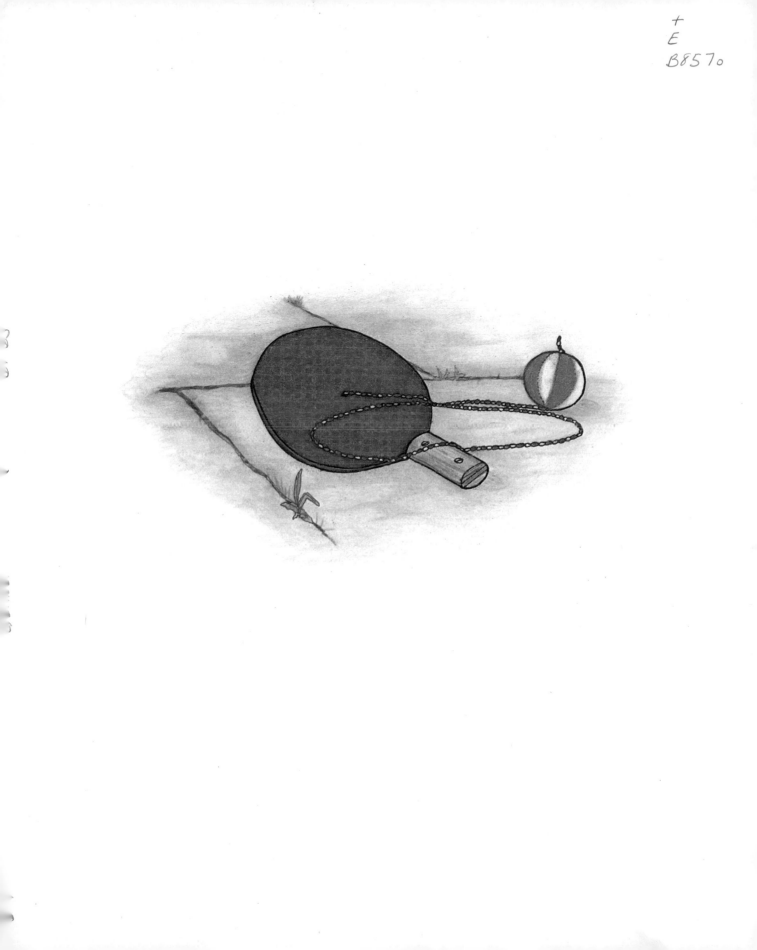

One bear all alone
Sitting by the telephone.

Two bears call to play,
"Will you come out for the day?"

Three bears on a train
To the sea and back again.

Four bears at the zoo
Waving to the kangaroo.

Five bears up a tree
One fell down and hurt his knee.

Six bears at the shops
Buying lots of lollipops.

Seven bears sharing sweets,
"Will you please save me some treats?"

Eight bears feeling sick
Someone take them home and quick!

Nine bears in the tub,
"Could you give my back a scrub?"

Ten tired bears have gone to bed.
Can you count each sleepy head?